THE UNICORN AND THE SECRET

A SACRED KNIGHT TALE

DAWN BLAIR

To Serenity,
Welcome to the secret.

Dawn Blair

Copyright © 2020 by Dawn Blair

All rights reserved.

This book is protected under copyright laws of the United States of America. No portion of this book may be reproduced in any form or by any electronic or mechanical means, including information storage and retrieval systems, without written permission from the author, except for the use of brief quotations in a book review.

The story and characters are entirely fictional. Any resemblance to actual events, persons (living or dead), or locales is purely coincidental.

Cover and layout copyright © 2020 by Morning Sky Studios
Cover design by Dawn Blair/Morning Sky Studios
Cover art copyright © Ateliersommerland |Dreamstime.com
Torch © Kretiw |Dreamstime.com

Books by Dawn Blair

Sacred Knight:

Quest for the Three Books
Manifest the Magic
To Birth a Destiny
History of a Dead Man (companion novella)
Prince of the Ruined Land

The Loki Adventures

1-800-Mischief
For Sale, Call Loki
For A Good Time, Call Loki
For More Information, Call Loki
For More Mischief, Call Loki
1-800-CallLoki (Omnibus of novellas 1-5)
1-800-IceBaby

Wells of the Onesong

Fractured Echo
Fall's Confession
The Doorway Prince
Stardust
Mystery of the Stardust Monk
Alexander's Den

Onesong

Tangled Magic

Ninjas

By the Numbers

Space Ninjas Aren't Real

Other short stories

The Last Ant

Broken Smiles

Oxygen

I'm With Cupid

Let's Make a Deal

Nonfiction

The Write Edit

90 Seconds to Courage

Children's Picture Books

Eggs at Play

THE UNICORN AND THE SECRET

Bound for greatness. Those words described Martias' friend, Steigan, perfectly.

Over the top of the gilded prayer book, Martias sat on the yellowing grass in the Temple courtyard watching Steigan, who sat on a wrought-iron bench nearby sharpening his short sword. The steady cadence of the whetstone singing against the metal blended with the lulling silence in the mid-afternoon. Martias wanted to forget his attempts at memorizing lines and merely stretch out over the ragged grass to find sleep. Blissful sleep which would take him away from the stillness of his everyday routine.

But the boy caring for his weapon a short distance away reminded Martias of the need for dedication, the sheering sound grating every so often and keeping Martias from falling into an after-lunch nap.

They were the only two out here enjoying the warmth of the final days of the harvest season. The breeze carried on it the scent of wood fires lit inside the Temple for heat. Martias wondered if any of the smell also came from houses in New

Lilinar across the lake. Humans had such a distaste of the cold.

But realizing that Martias would like company, Steigan often came with Martias to spend time outdoors. That compassion and dedication to their friendship put Martias ill at ease when he thought about the future.

It didn't matter that Steigan was an orphan; he had plenty of people around him who wanted him to succeed, including his mentor, Arlyn, and his adoptive parents, Sim and Lucinia.

Martias, on the other hand, had no one and was bound with a death sentence.

The centaur rose, snapping closed the prayer book he held. For a moment, he stared at the golden edges of the book before tucking it away in a leather pack he carried with him and cinched the ties closed. He couldn't sit here another moment pretending that his highest goal in life was to become a high-ranking sapere. His destiny had once been far different.

He stamped his dark hooves against the compressed ground, missing the spongy coolness of the forest floor. He needed to run. Just not into other centaurs. That thought made him feel so alone.

"Where are you going?" Steigan called out.

Martias rolled his head and shoulders. "I don't know. I just feel restless."

"Wait up." Steigan was already halfway to his feet, the whet stone slipped away in his pouch and sword sliding efficiently back into his scabbard. Every move spoke of the hours of training he'd had, probably ever since Arlyn thought he was capable of holding a wooden sword.

Martias sauntered over to the guardhouse by the drawbridge of the castle-like walls surrounding the Temple and its grounds. He picked up a bow and a quiver full of arrows that lay against the stone and slung it across his back. Then he started over the open drawbridge.

"Leaving!" Martias shouted back, already at a trot. Let the human run.

Steigan's pace picked up as he raced across the wooden bridge and octagonal causeway halfway between the Temple and the shoreline. Martias lengthened his stride a little more, then felt guilty for leaving Steigan behind. He stopped and waited as he reached the other side.

What he really wanted was time and space to run. Just some time alone, him and the pine trees. Maybe a night of frolicking in the moonlight. Just one night.

Martias turned. "Why don't you get a horse and we go out into the forest?"

"Why?" Steigan glanced around, but Martias didn't know what exactly his friend was looking for. "It's going to be time for evening prayer and training soon."

"We have plenty of time. Come on, Steigan. Let's just go out for a little while."

Steigan nodded, then began to smile. "All right. I'll be right back."

Martias watched as Steigan headed over to the stables and spoke to Kadlyn, the gamekeeper. They disappeared into the stables together and Martias' attention wandered back toward the forest. He hadn't seen another centaur for five cycles. Were there any tribes nearby, or were they all closer to the Palin Mountains now that the raining season had ended? Or had the fighting between New Lilinar and Plenelia scattered them? Had the battle disrupted their migratory patterns? Were the centaurs joining in and, if so, who's side were they taking?

"Let's go," Steigan called out behind him.

Martias heard, but he made no move until Steigan reined up beside him.

"Which way do you want to go?" Steigan asked, bringing the bay mare he rode under control, but Martias sensed the horse also wanted to run. Maybe there was something in the air. Or part of the changing of the seasons.

"Let's go to the east."

"There's no good roads that way. Why don't we head south."

Martias look south, hoping that Steigan thought he might be considering the option, but really he just wanted to roll his eyes in privacy. He knew that Steigan only wanted to go south to feel closer to Sim and Lucinia. Steigan was homesick.

As he was, yet he couldn't admit it.

Martias' back feet moved quickly as he turned his head, his long, curly brown hair flipping off his shoulder. "No roads. Let's just go out through the forest, just like Arlyn always did with us. Don't you miss that?"

It took a moment for Steigan to answer. "All right. Let's go to the east."

They headed around the lake where the Temple sat on an island in the center and into the town of New Lilinar. The streets were busy with people going about their afternoon business. Steigan saluted with his fisted hand over his heart to the domini on the street. Many ignored him as if they'd never seen him. Some did salute back. All seemed to ignore Martias.

The edge of the forest seemed to line right up with the final buildings of New Lilinar. One moment they were on the cobblestone streets, then they were on a small trail indented some into the earth made by people venturing out into the trees. The steep walls made by the walking of many two-legged people made it hard for those with four hooves to move along. After a short distance, once the trees thinned just a little bit more, Martias bounded off of the path and took to the flatter ground. Steigan fought the mare to keep her on the path for a bit longer before surrendering and letting her move off the trail.

"This way," Martias called out to Steigan with a large, circular gesture. "This way."

He guided Steigan deeper into the forest. The whole way he could hear his heartbeat quickening. A centaur, he just wanted to see one centaur in the distance.

A single glance to remind him he wasn't alone.

Steigan dismounted and started studying the area around them. "Look, there have been deer and rabbits moving through here. Lots of them. Do you think that all the domini moving into the mountains have scared them down here into the valley? Maybe the campfires..." He trailed off while he followed another set of tracks. Martias wished Steigan would announce he'd found cloven hoofprints.

Martias started forward again.

"Martias, we should be getting back," Steigan shouted behind him. "It'll be evening soon. We said we'd be back."

"Who did we tell?" Martias replied over his shoulder. No one knew they were gone, except maybe the gamekeeper. Only Kadlyn knew they had borrowed a horse and whatever else Steigan had told him. Probably not much, only that they would return the mare by evening. That wasn't much to go on.

"You said we'd go back."

Martias rounded back to Steigan. "Aren't you enjoying this? It's just like when Arlyn would take us both out in the forest. Let's stay out here for the night, just like we use to."

"We don't have food or blankets. And I've only got one waterskin that's barely half full.""

"We never had much when we were out with Arlyn either. He taught us to make do. Just one night. We've got time before sunset to get together everything we need to make it through the night."

His friend looked uncertain. Leave it to him to be the stick in the mud. Steigan, Goddess love him, was such a strait-laced person.

"Come on," Martias pleaded with a huge grin following it. "You know it'll be fun. It's not like they are going to beat you for breaking the rules."

"What about your duties at the Temple?" Steigan asked.

Martias felt his eyes narrow on Steigan. Was Steigan protecting him? He once again tried to smile it away. "No worries. Ever seen someone try to spank a centaur. Trust me, we won't get in trouble for this."

Steigan gave a surrendering sigh. "All right, but we head back at first light tomorrow. I don't want to miss too much training."

"Deal!"

Martias went out to see what there was in the surrounding area while Steigan began making a clearing for them to have a fire. The rainy season had ended and the growing season was beginning to make the days hotter, but the night remained mild. A low fire would keep the evening chill away.

While building the fire preoccupied Steigan, Martias headed deeper into the forest. He searched for hoofprints. Finding none, he took out his knife and carved the symbol of his family, a P with a lazy V at the top of it, into a tree. The shape of his V almost looked like a bird flying through the air. With it spread so wide, he decided to place an M above it all. Martias Pendorian. He placed another V above his M, highlighting the central slants of the M even more. He stood back, assessing his work. "Martias Pendorian, crown prince of the centaur Pendorian tribe," he whispered, knowing he could never say those words to any ever.

Anger rose through him and he began to slash at the marks he'd made on the tree. Over and over he cut the bark until the symbols looked like unrecognizable scratches. He would never be prince or chieftain of the tribe. He'd destroyed all hope of that."

"Martias?" came Steigan's voice through the trees. "You didn't get lost out there, did you?"

"Not lost," Martias called back.

"Not taking a piss, are you?"

Martias wondered if the word felt dirty in Steigan's mouth. "Nope."

Then Steigan was standing right beside him with a wide smile on his face. "Good. I'd hate to come upon that sight. There are just some things you can't unsee."

"Like you've never seen a horse pee."

"Yeah, but the horse isn't my friend. Trust me, it's different." Steigan waved his arm, encouraging Martias to follow. "Come on, I found a bunch of rabbits hiding in a bush. If we haven't scared them off, maybe you can hunt one down for our dinner tonight."

It wasn't long before Steigan showed him the rabbits and Martias downed one with an arrow. Shortly after that, they had it skinned and cooking over a spit spread across the fire.

Darkness crept across the sky, pulling in tight around their fire. One moon rose, keeping the sky a dark blanket cast over the trees. Martias looked up at the light scattering of stars above them. A second moon due to rise in the middle of the night, would soften the sky, but Martias knew Steigan would probably be asleep long before then. As much as Steigan had always loved being out in the forest with Arlyn, the air always made him sleepy. Many nights, Martias and Arlyn had stayed up much later, listening as the boy slept nearby. Martias wondered how Steigan would take it if he told his friend that he snored.

But tonight, Steigan stayed up with him. Did he sense how much Martias needed the companionship tonight? Martias hoped not.

"What do you think Arlyn's doing?" Martias asked, hoping to redirect Steigan's thoughts if they had been focused toward him. "Do you think he's out tracking Plenelians, circling around them in the dark?"

At first, the prospect seemed to excite Steigan, but then another thought intruded and dampened his mood. "I'd rather have him peacefully sleeping right now while on the road home to New Lilinar."

"He must be." Martias hoped his quick response would drag Steigan from the mood. "He's been gone for quite a while. Surely he is one of the domini coming home."

Steigan nodded.

Martias had overheard the saperes talking nearly a week ago that several domini were returning. He'd told Steigan about the news, but he wished he could promise that Arlyn was indeed one of those coming home. He'd left out the part about several of them being injured. Apparently, there were some dead among them too. More information he'd refrained from telling Steigan.

Granted, Martias had done that as much for himself as for Steigan. He needed Arlyn to return as much as, if not more, than Steigan did.

The pale moonlight cut through the trees like the Goddess' light, shaming Martias. He had no right to keep this knowledge from Steigan. It might be better if Steigan was braced for the possibility of losing Arlyn. Then there was his own faith brought to the forefront; the humans worshiped the Goddess, not the centaurs. Yet here, in the forest, he once again heard the old whispers of the earth calling him, deepening the teachings he'd had about the Goddess. Maybe the two weren't as disassociated as he'd once believed.

In their silence, the crickets began to chirp.

Steigan lay back and folded his hands beneath his head. "Why are we out here?"

"Because we decided to stay the night, for old time's sake."

Steigan turned his head, looking at Martias. "I know what you told me, but why are we really here? You've been distant lately, quiet. I just want to make sure everything's all right with you."

Martias had always thought that his father would send for him, tell him to come home. It had been five cycles. That hadn't happened. Nor had anything bad befallen him. "I'm fine," Martias lied. "Just needed a break. It's been odd with so many of the domini gone. It's stressing some of the saperes. Adonid--"

"What if he doesn't make it back alive?" Steigan blurted out.

"Adonid? He hasn't gone anywhere."

"No, Arlyn. What if Arlyn doesn't come back?"

Martias knew he had to say something. He felt only silence on his tongue, until he managed speak in a tiny voice, "He will."

He couldn't even be sure that Steigan heard him.

After a couple more moments, the crickets started again.

He knew he should tell Steigan that not all the domini were coming safely home.

Yet the little voice inside Martias screamed that Steigan already realized the truth.

As Martias turned his head and saw the firelight reflecting in Steigan's gaze, he also saw the fearful plea that Arlyn not be dead.

Steigan closed his eyes. Martias waited to see if Steigan would once again open them and have more to say, but Steigan didn't.

"It's going to be all right. He's on his way home," Martias

whispered as confidently as he could. Then he closed his eyes and drifted off to sleep.

"Time to get up, sleepyhead," was the next thing that Martias heard. He woke up to Steigan's booted foot nudging his hindquarters.

Martias squinted, not wanting to open his eyes yet. "It's not even morning."

"You said we'd leave at first light. Sun's rising. Let's go."

Martias let himself relax back down onto the forest floor, wishing it would soak him in. Even with Steigan moving around him, Martias hadn't felt this comfortable in a long time. The smell of dew on the plants and trees, mingled with the scent of earth, lulled him. "I don't want to go back," Martias said.

"We have to. I have training."

"No. That means you have to go back. I don't have to. I don't want to."

"You're going to stay out here in the forest?"

"I could."

Steigan pressed his boot against Martias again. "No, you couldn't. Come on. Get up."

Heaving a sigh, Martias sat up. "Yeah, there's no reason to be up yet." He plopped down on the other side and stretched out four legs.

"I could leave you. I marked the trail on our way out here, so you can follow that back whenever you want."

Martias rolled, twisting his waist around just enough to see Steigan. "You would leave me? I might get eaten by wolves."

"Then get up and let's get moving."

Martias clambered to his feet. "All right all ready. Breakfast?"

Steigan opened a pouch at his waist. "I have a bit of jerky, but that's all the rations I have." He handed a package wrapped with cheesecloth to Martias.

"You were holding out on me." Martias took a thin strip of dried meat and handed the rest back.

Steigan returned Martias' smile. "Yes, I was. I'd hoped to not need it. But let's face it, nothing out here is nearly ripe enough yet. If we wanted to stay out here, we'd have to work a lot harder and plan better."

"You want to stay out here?"

"No," Steigan snorted. "I was just saying if we did..."

"We could."

Steigan leaned back, all his weight on one foot. He put his gloved hands on his hips. "Why are you saying that?"

"Any day now, domini are going to be returning to New Lilinar for rest and supplies. Arlyn might be among them. Wouldn't it be neat to greet Arlyn."

"We don't know which way they are coming. They could be coming in on Traveler's Road rather than coming through the forest."

"Do you really want to go back to the Temple? Aren't you willing to admit that we're both bored to tears there? The domini who were left behind were left behind for a reason; they aren't very good. You are training them, and they know it." Martias wanted to add that none of the saperes were probably even missing the centaur right now. It seemed like they always thought him more trouble than he was worth. "Come on. Let's go."

The question played on Steigan's face as if he didn't understand it. "Go where?" he said finally and in a hopelessly slow tone.

"To the Palin Wars. Let's do this."

Steigan shrunk back. "I don't know."

"Do you really want to go back?" Martias asked, pointing

in the general direction of New Lilinar. "Or would you rather go find Arlyn and help him?"

Steigan's hands clenched and unclenched as he shifted his weight from foot to foot. "Arlyn. I want to go find Arlyn. I want to fight by his side."

"You sure? Because if we go, we go and we don't look back."

Steigan began nodding his head more vigorously. "Let's do this."

"All right."

With that, they started the trek toward the Palin Mountains where somewhere the domini were fighting back the soldiers of Plenelia.

Martias watched for signs of small animals as they walked, hoping to catch a rabbit or two for their supper. Anything to keep from having to eat the flower salad that Steigan was gathering up for them. As much as he knew that those same types of flowers were probably feeding his family's centaur tribe, he had become much more accustomed to the heavy, meat-laden meals made by the humans. He figured he had to be more bulked out than his brothers now, a result of no longer living the hunter-forager lifestyle. He'd really like to know if he was bigger than his eldest brother, Jepssa, now.

He'd probably never find out.

He silently wondered what would happen if they ran into a group of centaurs. The deeper they got in the forest away from New Lilinar and the closer they came to the Palin Mountains, the more likely it became that they would encounter at least some scouts. Would the centaurs they ran into even remember Martias? He'd changed a lot over five cycles and some memories were short. How many of the tribe actually remembered what happened when so few knew the truth to begin with? His father had shuttled him off to the humans pretty fast.

It took nearly five days to get to the base of the Palin Mountains and the ground got rocky and rough quickly. At least the diversity of the plants grew, so Steigan's flower salads had more variety. Meat also became more plentiful, though cooking it became a problem. The scent of the fire scared off game, and Steigan was afraid it would attract unwanted attention from any soldiers coming through the area. Until they reached the main camp where they figured Arlyn would be, they didn't want friend or foe finding out about them.

"This way," Steigan called out to Martias one afternoon. He pointed in the vague direction of the ground and let his finger drift upward in a general direction of the hill. "Footprints. Someone moved through this way."

"Do you see any of Arlyn's markers?"

Arlyn trained them to leave breaks in branches, often tending to spear a bent leaf over a twig in order to indicate the direction he was moving in.

"Nothing that looks like Arlyn," Steigan replied, bending down to examine a plant and the footprint left in the soil. "I am seeing a pattern though."

Martias leaned over slightly to inspect it, a boot print. If it wasn't a cloven hoof, Martias didn't care about it right now.

"But not one you recognize?"

"No."

"Could it be a Plenelian?"

They had never seen a Plenelian. For all they knew, the people who resided on the other side of the Palin Mountains next to the ocean had purple skin. Maybe a third eye. All Martias had heard about the Plenelians were that they didn't care for the obscure magical superstitions which lands like the far eastern kingdom of Dubinshire held onto. Still, the Plenelians had sent soldiers out to attack New Lilinar with some untrue claim about Holy Sapere Adonid working to bring magic back to the land. Fortunately, word came before the Plenelians got very deep into New Lilinar's territory and Adonid sent the domini out. To think what would have happened if they'd reached and attacked New Lilinar, taking the city unaware.

Martias shuddered at the thought.

"I don't know," Steigan answered, responding to Martias' question about the boot print being Plenelian. "There's no way to be certain right now."

Martias looked to the sky, pinpointing where the sun was in relation to the jagged horizon. "The sun's to be down long before we are used to because of the mountain. We should probably make camp soon. You got enough flowers for us for dinner."

Steigan grinned. "Don't tell me you're actually looking forward to it tonight?"

"I'm not, but I haven't seen a rabbit all day, I'm hungry, and I don't want to wake up famished in the morning."

After the sky had darkened as much as it would with the multiple moons in the sky, they went to sleep so that they would arise as soon as daybreak came. As they got further and further into the mountains, Steigan began sleeping in his armor against a tree, his sword sheathed but within reach.

"That can't be comfortable," Martias grumbled as they started their day. "You sure you're getting enough sleep."

"Easier and easier each day," Steigan responded, not looking in Martias' direction. "I have a sapere to guard and we are in dangerous territory now."

That lit an angry fire within Martias. He stomped right up to Steigan and pointed at the armor, his index finger slamming against it. "Nothing points us out as being from

New Lilinar more than this armor. Otherwise, we're just a couple of people hanging out in the forest."

Steigan's gaze rose to meet Martias'. "I won't disavow my allegiances just to keep myself safe. Besides, I can't leave it behind. I won't leave it behind. I'll need it when we reach Arlyn, if we're going to help him.

Martias softened at the thought of how much the armor meant to Steigan. Arlyn had given it to Steigan before heading out for the front lines. It had been the set of armor Arlyn had received when he became a dominus. Steigan had yet to earn the title, but everyone knew it would be soon. Rumor had it that he'd become the youngest person ever to earn the title of dominus.

"I know and I wouldn't expect you to abandon it." Martias stepped back from Steigan. "You ready to head out?"

Several times during that day, Martias recalled Steigan saying that he wouldn't disavow his allegiances and something about those words grated. Maybe it was because he was human, but Steigan always had had more faith. If he hadn't been an orphan, Steigan would have made a good sapere.

As night once again came upon them, Martias noticed the clouds floating awfully low in the sky. "It's going to be cold enough that we're going to have fog," he remarked to Steigan.

They made camp, then sat by the low fire trying to let the heat warm them thoroughly before they went to sleep. Martias continued to watch the clouds, enjoying the glimpses of stars he caught between masses. "What do you think they are, those pinpoints of light?"

Steigan glanced up for a moment. "I don't know. Can't say I've thought about it much."

"No one seems to." Martias pointed at the bright sliver of the moon. "Do you know that the centaurs have names for them?"

"Why would anyone name a moon? It's not like it's going

to respond to you calling out its name. It doesn't have special powers that will hear you."

Part of Martias wanted to take Steigan's words harshly, but at the same time, he knew Steigan was right. It was foolish to name the moons.

A cloud passed over the crescent. A moment later, the moon nearly disappeared behind the cloud. Martias noticed the red tint that marked other clouds only a short distance away.'

A scent, that of a fire burning, but different than their fire, drifted by him.

Martias rose. He heard Steigan move up beside him. "What's wrong?" Steigan asked.

The low clouds nearly engulfed the moon again.

"Something ill is on the wind tonight."

"What?"

Martias wanted to mention an old centaur tale about bad omens coming when the moon disappeared from the night sky, but he held his tongue. "The temperature drops quickly. You should sleep tonight with your back against mine."

"Yes, body heat would probably be good."

Martias sniffed the air again. The scent of the strange fire was now gone, and he hoped it was for good. "Come on. Let's get some sleep."

Martias lay down and settled while Steigan set the fire to continue its slow burn for a while longer, then Steigan came and sat down behind Martias. He leaned back against the dip in Martias' back. The armor felt cold, but the metal quickly warmed.

Feeling Steigan's breathing level out, Martias wondered how long it would take him to fall asleep. He watched the moon fade in and out behind the luminous clouds as he drifted off to sleep and thought of their own journey. The higher they climbed, the colder the nights had gotten. But something about tonight --

A scream pierced the silence of the murk.

Martias jerked awake, the fog he predicted now around them.

Steigan bolted upright, drawing his sword as he got to his feet. "Please tell me you heard that. I'd hate for my dreams to be trying to give me such a fright."

"I heard it."

Another shrill sound came through the trees as Martias was getting to his feet. It seemed to lock all four knees right beneath him. He watched Steigan take a step forward and listen. After a moment of Steigan gazing intently through the trees, he turned warily toward Martias. "I don't think that was human."

"Then what was it?"

Steigan's head shook side to side in short, sporadic jerks. "I don't know," he managed finally.

"I'd feel a lot better if you did."

"So would I."

They continued to stand, silent now, waiting for another of the shrieks which never came. But Steigan still looked on high alert and Martias sensed that his friend was listening for other sounds throughout the forest too. What was he hearing?

"I have to go look," Steigan announced.

"Do you want me to come with you?" Martias was certain that Steigan would admit that he didn't want a big, lumbering centaur to be following him as he tiptoed through the forest.

"Yes. I don't know what we'll find. It's probably nothing, but I'd rather that you were there to help than for me to have to wait for you to follow all my markers."

Martias nodded. He fetched the bow and arrows from

where he'd left them. He found Steigan ready to head out when he was.

"Let's spread out a few paces though," Steigan said. "We can canvas more area that way. Look for anything that could have been making that noise."

Martias nodded, then turned to head deeper into the forest away from Steigan. He reached out and snapped a branch, knowing it might be a breadcrumb for himself or Steigan to follow later. He just hoped that if there was something else out in these woods with them, that it wouldn't figure out their markers.

The forest grew very quiet and Martias soon could only hear the sound of his own hooves walking over the undergrowth. It crunched no matter how he tried to step. He knew many of the centaurs could walk unnoticed through the trees. Why couldn't he? Maybe this is why his tribe didn't want him back; he was noisy and clumsy. What good was a centaur that couldn't sneak up on its prey? Might as well have a target on his back.

His skills with the bow he held in his hand were far from legendary, but it had grown the friendship he had with Steigan. Nearly unstoppable with a sword in his hand, Steigan couldn't hit the stable wall at ten paces with a bow and arrow no matter how much Arlyn and Martias worked with him. Steigan had better luck throwing the weapons at his opponent. It was, quite frankly, the only think he'd ever known Steigan to completely fail at.

Martias began to hear voices through the thickening fog ahead and turned toward them. He knew he should go back for Steigan, but first he wanted a glimpse of what they'd be heading toward. If it were the domini, then there was no worry. But if they were Plenelian, then the scream had been a dire warning.

Martias began to wonder if it had been a ghost shouting

at them to flee. It wasn't like he'd never heard stories of this happening.

"Stop! The beast is already injured. Anymore and you'll kill it, then it'll be worthless," a man's awkward slur came through the trees.

Martias started toward the voice, afraid that he'd find a young centaur caught in a trap.

Sounds of bending branches and rustling leaves rushed toward Martias. A moment later, Steigan was there, putting a hand on Martias' chest. "You'll never guess what they've caught."

He expected Steigan's next words to be, "A centaur."

"Hush now, fool," said another man, his voice even more handicapped than the first as if he'd spent all night at the pub. "We don't need the whole carcass, just the long pointy thing."

"It's a horn, you lout!" There was the sound of a slap as if the first man had struck the second.

"Yeah, that thing."

No centaur that Martias knew of had a horn unless they were ceremonial, and then it was usually an impressive set of antlers.

"She's badly injured, but they are drunk," Steigan was saying. "I'd like to wait until they fall asleep, but she's bleeding. I think one of them shot her with an arrow."

Martias glanced down at Steigan. "What? Who? What are you talking about?"

Steigan's eyes rolled slightly as he took a deep breath before starting to explain again. "They have a unicorn. She's hurt. We've got to free her."

Steigan started to charge off as if explaining everything again had given him a plan. Martias grabbed onto his shoulder and held him back. "Steigan, it's a unicorn. The rest of the herd is probably around here somewhere. Let them gather their own."

Steigan turned shocked eyes toward Martias.

"They don't like interference," Martias explained quickly. "There are lots of them out there, but how often are they actually seen? Rarely, if ever."

"They've already abandoned her."

"How do you know that?"

"I don't know. I just do." Steigan's voice raised in irritation. Martias put up a hand to remind him of the need for silence. "I just do." The repeated words were quieter, but still paused and accented for emphasis.

Martias contemplated for a moment before shaking his head. He knew there was no way he would convince Steigan that the unicorns didn't want or need their help. But Steigan had never seen the distain the unicorns had for other races; the unicorns avoided nearly all humans at all costs. Centaurs, being half horse and half man, also collected the unicorn's discrimination, but not quite as fervently. "Trust me on this. The unicorns will take care of it."

"No, they won't." Steigan pulled free of Martias' grip. "She's been following."

There was something about Steigan's face that told Martias his friend was struggling with words he wasn't sure he should say. "What?"

Steigan's lips tightened. "She's been... trying to find me."

Martias laughed. "Trust me, a unicorn wants nothing to do with a human."

"Who's out there?" came one of the slurred voices.

At that, Steigan drew his sword and dashed off through the trees, leaving Martias behind. Martias cursed before following.

"Who are you?" shouted one of the men and Martias knew that Steigan had arrived in their camp.

Steigan said something, but with his back turned, the sound travelled in the other direction and Martias couldn't hear it amid the trees.

Martias knew his best bet would be to swing around and come in from the side while Steigan had them occupied. Martias hurried, knowing that in their drunken state the men couldn't hurt Steigan, unless there were enough of them to overpower his friend. He didn't remember if Steigan had given him a count of how many there were.

Moving around the perimeter, Martias lost sight of Steigan, who walked further into the enemy camp.

"Hey, kid, lost your mother, have you?" someone called out.

"I heard the scream and thought it might be her." Martias could almost hear Steigan shrug as he played their story.

"Scram," said a second person, the one who had called out at Steigan the first time. "Run along your way and forget what you've seen here."

"This is my unicorn. She's mine."

"No, she isn't. If she was, she's not anymore. Now get out of here."

Why hadn't they made note of Steigan's armor? It instantly called him out as being from New Lilinar. He was a long way from home.

"She's mine," Steigan cried out as if he was the little kid they believed him to be. "You can't have her."

Several men laughed.

"I won't let you," Steigan whined.

"Don't push your luck," Martias whispered as if force of will alone would let Steigan hear him.

"Get out of here, kid. Last chance," one of the men grumbled.

Martias came through the trees enough to see that Steigan had removed his armor, or at least the breastplate.

He had awkwardly tied his cloak around his waist. It looked bulky and barely hid the leg plates.

The men were closing in around Steigan, all brandishing weapons that didn't appear well cared for and scarred but could still kill.

"Not today," Steigan said. He pulled on an end of the tied cloak and the material came undone from around his waist.

One of the men rushed forward with his sword thrust forward.

Steigan pulled the breastplate up from where it had been collected in the cloak and used it as a shield against the attack. The blade struck. Metal deflected. The man went tumbling.

Steigan slung the armor on. His fingers worked deftly at fastening the buckles.

"He's from New Lilinar!"

"We're under attack."

Steigan hadn't completely secured his armor when they ambushed him once more.

"Hey, over here!" Martias called out, successfully making the men turn and giving Steigan the time he needed.

"We're surrounded."

Martias launched an arrow from his bow, striking the man in the shoulder. It spun him around and knocked him to the ground.

Steigan now had his sword out. "Surrender!"

"To kids?" asked the man who had attacked first as he picked himself up off the ground. "Is this how New Lilinar chooses to fight? By arming their children and sending them out?"

The other man, with a dagger in his hand, rushed for Martias.

It wasn't much more of a battle with the three men being barely sober enough to hold their weapons. Martias had only to defend himself long enough for Steigan to incapacitate them. But dragging the unconscious men to a tree for Steigan to tie up seemed like the most work that Martias had done. He couldn't meet Steigan's eyes, feeling ashamed that he'd left nearly the entire battle up to his friend while he merely blocked attacks. Saperes were not the ones to fight.

"It's all right," he heard Steigan say. For a moment, he thought Steigan might be talking to him, but then he saw Steigan sitting beside the frightened unicorn. He cut the hobble the men had placed on her legs. "Can you stand?"

The unicorn tried. She had several lacerations surrounded by dried blood. Some of them looked as if they were becoming infected.

"She can't move," Steigan said back over his shoulder to Martias.

"I don't want to be here when they come to," Martias said with a jerk of his head toward the bound men.

Steigan nodded, then turned back to the unicorn, He scooped his hands beneath her.

"You're not going to be able to lift her," Martias said. "You'll hurt yourself in trying."

"I can't leave her here."

"What are you going to do? Carry her?"

Steigan got that look and his shoulders stiffened with the resolve setting firmly in his mind. "If I need to."

"Oh, come on! Do you know how heavy she is?"

"I don't care. I will do whatever I have to." Steigan grunted as he lifted the unicorn into his arms and somehow got to his feet. He wobbled under the awkward weight. "Come on," he said, getting moving. Martias knew that once Steigan had started walking, it would be hard for him to stop.

"You're not going to climb the mountain carrying her. There's no way you'll make it up."

Steigan nodded. "You're right. We've got to go back down to the valley."

"Don't you think they will realize that's what we'll be doing? I understand you need to get her away. We'll go and make camp, get her fed and let her sleep. But she really needs to get back to the other unicorns. We certainly don't want them coming after us either. Trust me. We can only give her one night. Then we'll continue on our journey and the other unicorns can come take her back."

Steigan worked his way down the slope. "Maybe a day of rest will let her recover enough to walk with us."

Martias dropped his hands to his sides. "We don't want her with us. She needs to go back to her kind." He wished he could go home to the centaurs. Oh, how he envied this poor creature in Steigan's arms.

Not having any way of knowing if the men who had taken the unicorn had companions who would be searching for them, or how long it would take them to get free, Steigan and Martias went as far as they could before stopping. Steigan, fighting his own exhaustion, cared for the unicorn with gentle words while washing her down. She could barely stand for long, her spindly legs trembling the entire time.

"We should continue moving," Martias said finally. He found himself unable to stop looking back over his shoulder. "We're still too close and there's plenty of day left for us to travel."

Steigan glanced at the unicorn and his lips tightened. "I don't know if she can handle any more movement."

"Then leave her here." Martias gestured around them. "This is a sheltered area. We can set up a trail to lead them away from here if they can track us. We'll be faster by ourselves. She'll have plenty of time to rest."

"I'm not leaving her."

"You can't carry her any further. You aren't even going to

last until nightfall. We have to get out of here. Let's go and lead them away."

Steigan searched around the trees. "I can take them. Let them come. We'll make a stand here."

"Do you even have the strength left in your arms to draw your sword out?"

Steigan's angry face tightened even further. He reached across and made to pull his sword from its scabbard. He only made it about halfway before his hand released the hilt. He let out a shocked breath as the metal slid back into the sheath. He stared at his gloved hand as if it had betrayed him.

"You're tired," Martias said.

"A dominus shows no weakness."

"You're not a dominus yet. If you let that horned horse weaken you further, you won't ever get your title because those men will overtake us."

Steigan glanced down at the unicorn. After a moment of awful silence, Steigan turned. "You could go on without us."

Martias felt as if he'd been struck. "Yes, I suppose I could." Hadn't that been what he'd really wanted when he had left New Lilinar? He made to leave but stopped with a heavy stomp of his hoof. "What can I do to help?"

Steigan smiled. "If I carry her weight across my shoulders, I can probably go faster. Help me get her on my back."

Martias shook his head, but he went over to Steigan. "This is a bad idea. Those bony legs of hers are likely to hit you in the face."

"No, she won't. She'll be calm. I don't know how, but I just know she will." Steigan knelt down beside the unicorn and took her head in his hands. "She's not afraid."

Martias kept himself from telling Steigan once again that she needed to go back to the herd, that it would be best for her, and that Steigan had no idea what she was really thinking or feeling. He'd made the decision to help Steigan, so he would. "Let's get her up again."

It took a couple tries and Steigan had to walk with a bend in his back, but soon they were heading down the mountain once more. They walked until evening.

Steigan put the unicorn down and stretched out. "Can you make a low fire and set up camp? I want to circle back." He looked off into the woods, his head giving a light shake. "I have a feeling they heard us arguing and have been following. I want to lead them away."

"Sure," Martias said, rolling his eyes. "Now you want to lead them away."

"Keep the fire low. If you can find some soft ground to dig a pit, that would be preferable. I'd hate for them to see the flames."

"I've got this," Martias said. Not only did he have some wilderness training with Arlyn, but he had lived for many years with the centaurs. Just because he'd been cast out didn't mean that he'd forgotten.

He watched Steigan go, knowing his friend had to be exhausted. Then he started to make camp for the night.

The unicorn tracked him, her big, dark eyes seemingly filled with curiosity.

"What are you staring at?" Martias snapped. "I hope you aren't going to get us both killed." He stared right back at the small beast, crossed his arms across his chest, and continued his glare until the unicorn looked away. Victorious, he went back to his preparations.

Until he noticed the animal watching him again.

"What?"

The unicorn gave a soft nicker.

"Don't try charming me. I may look similar to you," Martias said, twisting at the waist and indicating his long back, "but you and I have nothing in common other than four legs and hooves."

She made another noise.

"Okay, yes, you want to be Steigan's friend too. I guess we also have that in common." He stopped, realizing that he had understood the unicorn. He felt his feet moving him at an awkward sideways step.

It had to have been his imagination.

Hurried footsteps broke his thoughts and Martias pulled his bow from his back, notching it nearly in the same movement. He pulled the arrow on its string back to his chin, sighting down the shaft.

Steigan came through the bushes. He put his finger to his lips, then pointed to his eyes, then back into the forest.

Walking sideways so he could keep watch on the way he'd come through the trees, Steigan moved closer to Martias. "There's two of them, very drunk," Steigan whispered. "I doubt they will find us if we are quiet."

Martias nodded. For as much as he wanted to stay safe, he wasn't certain he could release the arrow even to strike down an enemy. He had no desire to watch someone die, not again. His fingers began to tremble and he half feared he might prematurely release the arrow.

No sounds came from the forest.

He trained to be a sapere. They weren't fighters. No, that was the domini; Steigan trained to be a warrior, to kill people. Martias would wear robes of white and bless people, lead them through confused times and emotions back toward the steady ground lit by the Goddess' light. Steigan would defend. Martias knew his friend hadn't killed anyone, not yet at least. He figured that time did come. How would Steigan react? Would he panic? Would he cry to Arlyn?

No, Martias doubted that Steigan would show weakness. That wasn't in the nature of a dominus.

But Steigan would feel it, dream about it, much as Martias was always haunted against his will. He would never forget the tragedy of losing his older brother.

"They must have turned, gone the other way," Steigan said.

Martias lowered the bow, gently releasing the tension on the string until he could safely pull the arrow off. He stowed the arrow in his quiver and slung his bow across his back once more. He busied himself with settling things around the camp so he wouldn't have to look at Steigan. Had he really intentionally dragged his friend out here into this, toward the battle, where people were getting killed? Shame flooded him and the more he thought about it, the worse he felt.

"I'm sorry," Steigan said, collapsing down on the ground by the young unicorn. "I haven't gathered anything for us to eat today."

"You've been carrying her all day. How could you?" Martias tried to make it sound as if he was forgiving Steigan without actually saying the words. He really should be doing the apologizing rather than it being the other way around. "I haven't been hunting either,"

"I don't have the energy to cook or eat. If you're hungry, I have some more rations in my pack. It's not much." Steigan already looked half asleep,

"I'm fine," Martias lied. He needed more to eat than most humans, and he'd already been sacrificing. What had he been thinking in leading Steigan out this way without any supplies?

He had hoped his friend would call him an idiot and abandon him. He knew he deserved no less. But Steigan had remained faithful, a more trustworthy soul than any other Martias had ever known. Now, Steigan would keep this unicorn safe for as long as he had to. A shield. A protector. Steigan was both of those things. Bound for greatness.

What could Martias say about himself? Murderer? Pretender? Outcast?

Had he subconsciously wanted to make Steigan all those things too?

Suddenly, he was no longer hungry either.

Keeping the painful thoughts to himself, Martias lay down on the other side of the fire and set about forcing himself to go to sleep.

He woke sometime later feeling cold and wet. Brushing at his arms, he realized he was covered with slick moisture. At first, he imagined it to be blood, but the texture too thin and the lack of smell made him realize it couldn't be. Reaching over with a long branch, he stoked a dim glow from the fire. Their camp was touched by a light dusting of snow.

Glancing to Steigan, he saw his friend and the unicorn covered in a blanket of frozen white. Steigan lay shivering, his back against the unicorn's.

"Steigan," Martias called out. "Steigan, wake up."

Steigan trembled but didn't rouse.

Martias reached over and shook Steigan.

Steigan came up with a dagger in his hand. Martias drew back, avoiding the lashing swipe.

"It's me," Martias said as Steigan's wide eyes tried to focus.

"Martias? What's wrong?"

"Snow."

Realizing there was no immediate danger, Steigan lowered his weapon. "Snow? That's why it's so cold."

"Yes." Martias pointed to the unicorn. "None of us should be sleeping right now. We might not wake up."

"Can we build up the fire, or is the wood too wet?"

"I'll see what I can do. You try to warm her up. She's too young to be this cold. She's used to having her mother, probably the whole herd around her."

Steigan gave a small smile of appreciation, then went to

the unicorn. He woke her up as he sat down beside her, then pulled her into his lap. Her spindly legs stuck out, but she seemed fairly limp. Martias hoped it wasn't already too late. He ramped up the fire, knowing that the flames coming out of the pit he'd dug last night would be a signal if the men were still searching for them. He had no choice though; they all needed to warm up. Hopefully, the snow caused the other camp to huddle down too.

As it got closer to morning, the wind began to pick up. The fire raged, seeming to lick out frantically at the unseen breeze.

Steigan brought the unicorn closer to the fire and lay down beside her. Martias sat behind them, trying to shield them from the wind's growing anger. He watched the snow mounting, partially from the flakes falling out of the sky and the rest being what the wind drifted around the trees.

Martias' muscles felt so stiff from shaking. If they all died here, he'd be the one to blame.

The nagging thought finally made him stand. He couldn't sit here any longer. He had to do something.

"Where are you going?" Steigan asked, sitting up.

"Just walking," he lied. "I'll be back shortly,"

"Shout if you need anything," Steigan said.

Martias nodded, then headed into the forest. He should leave them. He hadn't brought good luck to them. What had he been thinking? Steigan had learned enough about wilderness survival from Arlyn to keep them alive for a few days, but not for weeks, and certainly not with a unicorn in their care.

Quickly deciding that he needed to find the unicorn herd so that they could take the youngster back, Martias began to search for signs. Everything looked the same, especially in the snow.

"You'd think I'd at least be able to find tracks. Nice hoofprints. Come on." He continued walking.

The snow came well over his hooves now.

"Goddess, why did you give me the urge to come out here?" he asked. "Why did you let Steigan come with me? Is it your intent that I send him to Gohaldinest? Why must I bear that on my consciousness? Why do I bring death to those around me? What is it you request of me?"

Martias let his questions fall silent so that he could listen for an answer. Only the wind made small sounds coming through the tree leaves, and in none of it could Martias decipher an answer of any sort.

"Do you even hear me, Goddess?" He spoke his question louder than he had those spoken before. His voice echoed through the trees. "Why not punish me alone? What did I do that was so awful?"

He closed his eyes. He knew the answer to that: he'd worked magic: an offense against the Goddess. For that, his soul would never be clean. No matter how much he cried for forgiveness, or how much he prayed as a sapere. He could spend the rest of his life repenting, but it would never be enough.

Yet obviously his misdeed was so strong that those around him were bound to suffer and die.

"What can I do?" he whispered. "I want to make it right. What will gain your forgiveness?"

A glint of light through the trees caught his eye and he turned in time to see the sun coming out from behind stormy clouds. The snow had stopped falling, but left everything shimmering with its coat of winter as the light turned the sky a brilliant pink and yellow. Something about the shape of it made him recall the sunburst collar that the Holy Sapere wore during important ceremonies.

The Goddess wanted him to become the Holy Sapere.

Certainly, if he was Holy Sapere, consort to the Goddess, she would speak to him, soothe his wounds, and clear him from all the guilt he held.

But could a centaur reach such a high position?

If he could, that would be proof that the Goddess was forgiving him. He wanted that more than anything.

Martias looked back and saw that his tracks through the snow had been blown over by the wind, covering his trail. "This is a path I must walk alone," he said, understanding and nodding. He looked back to the part of the sky where the sun's brilliant rays still shone brightly. "This is for me to do. But I must find my way back to Steigan. I won't abandon him to fate. He will be there to see me succeed. I can't do this without him. He's been my only friend."

Martias stood there looking out over the part of the valley he could see. Steigan had no choice in being a dominus; being left as an orphan insured that he would gain no higher title. In times of war, like this with the Plenelians, a dominus would be sent to battle with no assurance that they would return. Like Arlyn. Only because Steigan hadn't yet gained the title of dominus kept him from being sent out.

But Martias had brought him out here anyway, a place where Steigan shouldn't yet be. Goddess, he had led his friend to battle. What if they had found a larger party of Plenelians rather than some scoundrels who wanted to make a profit from selling the pieces of a unicorn.

Even knowing his fate, Steigan had always strived to be the best dominus that he could. He neither doubted what he was doing nor rued his lot in life. His only fault, if Martias really had to look for one, was that Steigan spent so much time with Arlyn that he didn't make regular friends. Arlyn had done everything he could to make sure that Martias and Steigan stayed close.

Did Arlyn regard Martias the same way that the older dominus believed in Steigan?

A flood of warm consideration went through Martias. Tears came to his eyes and made his nose tingle even more than it did from the cold. "Goddess, why didn't I see that? Have I been so blind until now?"

Martias turned and started rushing back toward camp. He couldn't wait to tell Steigan that they should be on their way home. He wouldn't tell Steigan why he'd come to that decision, only that they should.

Then, the ground gave way beneath Martias.

He screamed with surprise as he fell. It seemed like part of his body went one way while his legs went another. His hooves dug into snow with slick mud beneath as they slid out from beneath him. He rolled several times.

"Martias!" he heard Steigan shout from somewhere through the trees. "Martias!"

Martias came to a dizzy stop and, as the ground settled around him, he saw the thick tracks he'd made sliding down the mountain. He felt leaves and mossy plants clinging to him. His entire body felt marred by wet slime.

A moment later, Steigan came into view making his way down the hillside. Several times his hand touched the ground so that he could stay upright while half sliding, half tripping down the slick terrain.

"Careful," Martias tried to tell Steigan, but the word came out garbled, as if he had spoken right through a mouthful of this mud.

Steigan's gloves, boots, and pants were covered in it by the time he got down to Martias. "Stay still," he said, hastily wiping off the dirt on his thighs before putting his hands on Martias.

"I'm fine. Just give me a moment for the world to stop spinning, then help me up," Martias stated.

"Let's make sure you'll be able to stand before we try. That was a nasty fall you took. What were you doing?"

"Walking! Clearing my head, just like I told you." He paused. Then, in a much calmer tone, he said. "Actually, I was thinking we should head home. The domini could be anywhere and these hills are awfully big. It's amazing that we found anyone at all, and it would be silly if we stumbled into the enemy again."

"But, Arlyn..."

"Will be heading home soon, I'm certain. Look, if he found out we were out here as ill-prepared as we are, he'd smack our heads right off our shoulders." Martias tried to lift himself up as he felt Steigan run a hand over his leg. "I mean, if either one of us got injured, we'd be in a sorry state."

Steigan shot him a humored look.

"I'm fine."

"Yes, you and your four left feet. Stay still a moment longer."

"Really, this isn't--" Pain tore through Martias and he screamed. He was pretty certain that anyone on the mountain had heard him. It took him a good length of time to get his breath back. "Goddess, what did you do that for?"

Steigan shook his head. Martias felt him still holding onto the leg. The fact that Steigan couldn't look him in the eye wasn't good. Steigan could see something and wasn't telling Martias.

"Come on. Help me to stand up," Martias said one last time.

"It's not broken," Steigan said.

"But?"

"But you've definitely sprained it. You shouldn't be putting any weight on this for a good, long while."

"We can't stay here," Martias said.

"I could try to go for help, but that could be days and you have no way of getting food or water for yourself."

"Not to mention the unicorn."

Steigan swung his gaze around. "There's a ledge down there a ways. It doesn't look like it's too far until we get beneath the snow line. We're probably right in a spot that got a bit of snow and rain. Let's get you to the ledge, then I'll come back up for Tyana."

"Tyana?"

"Yes." Steigan gave a shy smile. "I've named her that. She seems to like it."

"Please tell me you're not planning on taking her back to New Lilinar and keeping her as a pet," Martias said. "The last thing they want is another four-legged creature running around the halls and your room at the annex is certainly not big enough for a fully grown horse, let alone one with a horn."

Steigan chuckled as he stood up. "Agreed! One person with four left feet is all they need at the Temple. Now, let's get you up. Don't put any weight on that leg."

It took several tries before Martias rose off the ground. The first few times, he slipped and they thought he might just slide all the way down to the ledge. Even though Steigan joked about it, Martias wondered if it might be better if he did. Then, flinging mud all over each other, Martias stood and clung to Steigan for support. Using Steigan as a crutch, Martias made his way down to the ledge.

Steigan was panting heavily by the time they reached it. He leaned forward, hands on his knees, and tried to catch his breath after getting Martias settled.

Steigan went back up the hill and brought down snow in both his hands. "Here, put this around your ankle, let it melt away."

"Goddess, that's cold!" he complained, but he didn't pull his leg away.

"We're going to have to take this slowly," Steigan said. "Rest here while I go back for Tyana."

Martias watched Steigan climb back up the way they had come down. Then he had to wait. It seemed like forever before he saw Steigan returning with the unicorn.

"Ready?" Steigan asked when he got down to the ledge where Martias was. He once again carried the unicorn in his arms.

"You do realize that there is no way you are going to be able to help me off this mountain while carrying her, don't you?"

"Let me worry about that. If I have to take both of you down, one at a time, a little ways then come back for the other, I will do that. Let's try it this way first, since going down at once would be the best, but we'll see what happens."

"You are one stubborn person, you know that?" Martias asked.

Steigan shrugged. "What other choice do I have?"

The words rang in Martias' head while they headed down. He'd really been hoping that Steigan would give him a flippant answer, possibly even something about how one needed to be stubborn when dealing with Arlyn, but Steigan had chosen his other words instead. *What other choice do I have?*

Life hadn't given Steigan another option. Steigan had been abandoned on the Temple steps, an act which sealed his fate right there. With no family, money, or other means of support, an orphan would not be put into the sapere track, but rather would be trained to be a dominus, and his life forfeit for the sake of the Temple should the need arise. Arlyn's favorite statement was that a dominus showed no weakness, so it stood to reason that Steigan would follow that through to the letter. He wouldn't ask for help. He had no other option but to make it through whatever the task was before him.

Steigan found a stream of cold water running through it as they neared the end of the day. He filled their water skins and soaked the ends of his cloak in it. After suggesting that they make camp a short distance away, Steigan wrapped the damp cloth around Martias' ankle. Then he took care of the unicorn.

"I'm sorry," Steigan said as the day began to darken. "There were fish in the stream, but I couldn't catch one."

"It's fine. I hurt too much to think about eating anyway."

Steigan's look spoke his disbelief. After a moment, Steigan lay down beside the unicorn and soon began lightly snoring. He'd exhausted himself today.

The next two days were more of the same, except that Steigan suggested that they stop to rest in areas where there was plenty of edible vegetation. After two days without much food, even the natural salads were beginning to taste good. Each night, Steigan fell quickly to sleep.

On the third day, they woke to the unicorn moving around their camp. Martias had opened one eye at the sound of crunching leaves to find her walking the perimeter. He shifted to watch, wondering if she was getting ready to take off.

Steigan bolted upright and rolled to his hands and knees.

"What's she doing?" Martias whispered.

Remaining crouched, Steigan turned as Tyana passed the boundary. "Something's out there."

"The herd she belongs to?"

"No."

"The men we took her from?"

Martias found both the unicorn and Steigan turning to

look at him. An oddly unsettled pulse ran up his back and shook through his shoulders.

"No," Steigan said. "This is... worse."

"We should move on then," Martias said, already maneuvering so Steigan could get him up. The unicorn stood between them and the forest while Steigan helped Martias to his feet.

They walked in silence for a good length, the unicorn behind them. Every so often, Tyana would pause to glance back. Each time and, as Martias noted, just slightly before her hesitation, Steigan slowed in his steps as if waiting for her approval to continue on.

"Is she communicating with you?" Martias asked.

"The unicorn, no," Steigan answered.

"You could have fooled me," Martias whispered under his breath. He wasn't sure if Steigan heard him or not, because just then Tyana made Steigan look back and crane his neck trying to look back through the forest. Then, as if they were of one mind, the two started moving again. Martias shivered.

At least with the unicorn now walking on her own, Steigan only had to assist Martias and they made much better progress down the mountainside during the day. Shortly before nightfall, they made camp.

Tyana stood at the perimeter once again. If Steigan moved, she adjusted her position.

"Are you sure it's not the herd she belongs to?" Martias asked again.

"Positive," Steigan said, pausing for only a moment as he tossed kindling on the fire.

Martias wondered if it was a centaur stalking them through the woods, but he knew that was hopeful pride talking. He pushed the thought away.

Martias lay away throughout the night, listening each time the unicorn got up to pace the invisible boundary of their camp. Steigan slept soundly through it, not noticing even when she returned and dropped down close to him once more.

The next day followed much the same pattern, except that Steigan seemed to breathe heavier. He didn't seem to walk as fast.

"When we get back," Martias said, "I'm going to be the best sapere I can be."

"That's nice," Steigan answered.

"No, really. You've worked hard to be a dominus and here you are not giving in. You've inspired me. I want to do more, be more."

"Um-hmm," Steigan muttered non-committedly.

Disappointment overtook Martias. He'd been hoping for a more reaffirming response. His emotions were crushed enough that he remained silent for the rest of the day. Fortunately, Steigan called it quits in the late afternoon and they began to set up camp. He had barely gotten the fire set, something becoming increasingly unnecessary as they went further down into the warmth of the valley now, when Tyana dropped to the ground and Steigan landed not too far away. Both were asleep in moments.

At least they hadn't been watching behind them all day.

As Martias sat close to the fire and watched them sleep, he found himself smiling. Steigan had worn himself out. It wasn't that he wasn't supportive of Martias' new commitment, but he just had no energy for it right now. Maybe it was something that Martias needed to believe in himself, rather than getting outside validation. Steigan had never doubted his own abilities and never begrudged the conditions of his life. Was this unicorn his reward for faith?

Or a bad omen in a beautifully clever disguise?

Martias wondered why his trust always waivered. What did that say about him?

Did it make a difference if one were an orphan rather than being abandoned by their family? Either way, the ensuing results were the same: a child left to the mercy of the world.

Martias leaned forward, placing his head against his hands. "Goddess, what am I going to do?"

He wished for the answers to come to him in his dreams that night. By morning, he hoped to have resolved all his misgivings.

Disappointment flooded him as soon as he felt the sunlight on his closed eyelids. Realizing he was waking in the morning and no answers revealed themselves inside his mind, he started to rise for the day.

A black shadow off to his right moved.

Martias didn't have his feet beneath him when something slammed into his head. He teetered, swaying uncomfortably. He felt blood spilling over his cheek. He couldn't see what moved in front of him. A moment later, a punch contacted on his other cheek.

Blackness welcomed him once more.

When he woke again, his feet were tied together and his hands bound behind his back. A rope around his neck acted like a collar. Lying on his side, he couldn't move to look at anything around him.

He saw legs as the feet beneath them moved into view. At first, the person walked around Martias, but then turned swiftly toward him. A small cloud of dirt kicked up in the spin.

Martias tried to look up, but with the position that his arms were in from his hands being collared to him, he couldn't see all the way up the person. Only ragged leggings and the tattered end of a tunic.

"So, centaur, what brings you out here? Little far from your herd, aren't you?"

"Tribe," Martias answered, finding his mouth incredibly dry. "We're not horses."

"I think if I called you a horse, you'd be a horse. Not much choice where you're at."

Martias stayed silent, but he half hoped to hear sounds of Steigan nearby. Only half, because the other part of him hoped his friend had escaped with Tyana. Then, there might be a rescue underway. Besides, if he didn't say anything, he couldn't irritate his captors. He suspected these were not friendly people around him.

The man moved around behind Martias. The sound of footsteps stopped. A moment later, a hand smacked against his flank. "Now see here, that's some strong horseflesh."

Martias tried to turn, attempted to flip, find any movement he could make against the bonds, but he discovered none.

"If you keep moving like that, you're going to injure yourself. I can't have that happen, so you just stay still." The man's hand moved over Martias. "You'll be allowed to stand when we are ready to go."

Martias continued to fight. "What if I won't remain still?"

"Then we'll bind you to the ground with tethered ropes. At least this way you have some range of movement."

"I need to go pee."

"Well, for now, you've got to hold it. Stay still and you won't notice it as much."

The hand tapped twice more against his flank before a weight pressing down onto his hip told Martias that the man was standing up.

Martias held still, not because he'd been told to or because he needed to relieve himself, but more because it made it easier to hear what was going on around him. He listened to the man walk around behind him, out of Martias' sight. Martias' stomach gurgled, a sound which annoyed him because it not only blocked the other noises around him, but the tingling ache distracted him. He didn't have much room to look around, but he used the range he had. The muddy ground indicated he hadn't been moved far if at all. The area had been well trampled, meaning either there was multiple men or Steigan had been up and moving around before Martias woke. The fact that he heard no sounds of struggling or the man talking with someone else, indicated that Martias might be out here alone.

Had Steigan abandoned him?

What a horrible thought! But what else could Martias believe? Steigan should be here, swinging his sword and defending his sapere. Instead, there was no indication that Steigan was anywhere nearby.

Maybe it was possible that Steigan was sleeping. But the man hadn't told Martias to keep his voice down, nor had his voice been restrained as if trying to keep someone from waking.

Unless Steigan was tethered to the ground. That would be the only way that Steigan wouldn't give a fight. Did the man have a way of silencing the unicorn too? Or had Tyana run away?

So many questions, and yet Martias had answers to none of them.

For once, he truly felt fear.

As he lay still trying to listen for any sounds, all he could hear were the sounds of heavy boots as people walked around him. Martias thought there might be three of them. They spoke quietly among themselves ever so often and it sounded to Martias like they might be waiting for someone. But they never spoke to anyone else, Martias hoped Steigan had escaped. Was that who they were waiting for? A member of their party who had gone out searching for Steigan? His friend was quite the climber. Steigan could be up a tree and watching from the branches before they even thought to look up. No one ever did. Steigan remarked that it was a flaw in humans that they never thought anything could be above them.

Martias tried to turn his head, but all he could see was the crook of his elbow.

"Something has happened," one of the men said. "He's not coming back."

"All right. Get him up," said another.

"You should cut out his tongue while he's down. We might not have another chance," the third man put in.

"Someone might want him to speak."

"No one wants a mule that speaks," the third man said in a mocking tone to the other. "They don't want input from their livestock."

Martias found himself getting tense as three sets of human feet stalked toward him. All he could do was to bend his elbows in together, which opened up the expanse of his chest. The extent of his protection didn't leave him feeling very safe. He could close his eyes, but that had never done him any good. Just because he couldn't see reality didn't mean it wasn't there.

He had learned that when he prayed over the shattered body of his dying brother.

"Come on, centaur. Open your mouth and don't give us any trouble."

Martias glared at them.

"Maybe he don't understand you."

The man Martias had seen before leaned in. "He knows what I'm saying. He just hasn't realized that he's our slave. You hear that, centaur? You a slave now. Which gives you a choice: you can either do as we say and we find a nice owner for you, or you can rebel and we sell you to the meanest, cruelest person we can find."

Martias saw the blade of a knife coming closer to his face.

"What's it going to be?"

Martias thought about telling them he was a centaur prince, but why would they believe him? They'd probably all then claim that they too were princes. Maybe a king of some land. Even if they did believe him, no tribe would backup his claim, nor would the centaurs save him. He decided to remain silent.

"Last warning."

"I am a sapere from New Lilinar," he said quickly, followed by snapping his mouth tightly shut.

At least as they laughed, the knife pulled away from Martias' face.

"What good is a sapere out here?" one of them asked, but Martias didn't know which one, not that he'd seen anyone other than the one man. "Shall we bow to the Goddess and hope she doesn't throw lightning down upon us?"

"Oh, let us bow," another of his captors mocked.

"No centaurs living with the humans," the last man said. "That's pure malarkey. Can't imagine that happening for very long. Cut out his tongue before he starts preaching to us."

Several hands grabbed onto Martias. He tried to close his elbows together.

Instinctively, he closed his eyes.

Fingers pried into his cheeks as they tried to dig into his mouth.

One of them grabbed onto his hair and pulled his head back.

He hated being helpless.

He was losing.

"Coom ra wialca do," he said as they won the war to get their fingers into his mouth. He might as well say it one last time. "Sha belika nee."

The assault stopped as the men retreated.

Martias was only partially aware of it. "Ha ne," he continued.

"He said he was from New Lilinar."

"That one guy that we took to Lord Irragon... do you think?"

"What? That he taught a stray centaur?"

"Nah. Come on, take out his tongue. We'll take him to Montikovert."

Martias once more felt the pressure on him as they tried once again to get to his face.

"Hold him down."

Turning his head, Martias resisted as much as he could. He didn't have much leeway.

"Twist him. Put your leg on his shoulder."

Martias squeezed his eyes shut, trying to scrunch his whole face against them.

What would his tribe think if they could see him now? What would his father say? These thoughts squeezed into his mind and he wished they hadn't. HIs father had abandoned him, left him to die at the hands of the humans. What did it matter if it was the dagger of the Holy Sapere of New Lilinar or the knife of these ruffians?

But he wouldn't lose his tongue. He would make them kill him.

He began to thrash. His legs, still bound together, swung like thick sticks as he tried to roll over. The men jumped away, getting to a safe distance.

One of them laughed. "Good. He's a strong one. Selling this one will be lots of fun."

Martias heard them moving in around him again and he resumed his fight. Where was Steigan?

"Grab onto him there!"

Martias pulled his arms apart. He couldn't break the rope,

but it tightened around his throat. He would either strangle himself or make them cut the cord.

Someone noticed. "He's suffocating himself."

"Grab a branch and knock it against his head. This'll be easier if he's unconscious."

A bright flash of colors brightened his vision as a thick piece of wood smashed into his head. To his surprise, he didn't fall unconscious. He couldn't see much of anything and being deprived of air wasn't helping things. Sporadic flashes swam in his sight.

"Give me that."

"Don't!" the third man yelled. "If you hit him again, you might kill him. He's no use to us if he's dead." The man stalked toward the others and, a moment later, Martias heard the piece of wood crash through the branches of a bush a short distance away. "You and your bright ideas."

A man knelt down beside Martias, seized the ropes, and held it so Martias couldn't keep the ever-tightening pressure on it. Martias gasped and began to cough as breath entered his lungs once more.

"How does a sapere know the old rites?" he asked.

"I was taught them."

"Who taught you?"

Martias almost admitted to it. Then he remembered the larger goal at hand here. He looked up into the man's pock-marked face. "Your mother."

For an instant, the man's face turned red. Then he smirked, realizing what Martias was up to. "All right. Have it your way. We can come back for you."

He stood up and turned to the other men. "We leave him here. Two days, and he'll be quite ready to go with us. Pray, sapere. Pray all you want, but your goddess isn't coming to get you out of this one."

"What if he tries to choke himself again?" one of the men asked.

"He falls unconscious and his arms relax, loosening the ropes. Don't worry. There's not much he can do. No food, no water. Two days and he'll be glad to see us coming back."

They walked away. Martias realized they must not know about Steigan at all, since they never mentioned someone coming along to release the centaur.

Martias breathed relief. All he had to do was wait for Steigan to return. But where had he gone? Why had he left without a word? Would he come back?

The tension grew inside him as the men's footsteps down the hillside faded and silence returned to the forest. He'd really been hoping to hear from Steigan by now. Any moment.

Still nothing.

It gave Martias a moment to reflect on all that had happened.

What exactly *had* happened? He'd been asleep and awoken to be captured. It felt like he missed pieces to the puzzle. Worse, his head ached from the blows he'd taken.

The morning grew late and turned to afternoon, then evening. Martias tried to wiggle free, but the most he managed to do was to spin in circles. In doing so, he realized his ropes were tied to nearby trees.

"Why did Steigan leave?" he whispered.

The trees had no answer for him.

He wanted to call out for Steigan, but he knew the men wouldn't be far. Maybe they were even hiding away, thinking that the centaur had companions nearby. Would they suspect a human friend coming to his aid, or would they hope for more centaurs to enslave?

Martias knew the way the trees of the forest deadened

sound. It would be possible to call out and no one might hear him at all.

But, did he have to sound like a human?

Martias blew air through his mouth, making his lips flap.

What if there were other centaurs around? What if they heard him? He'd be just as helpless to centaurs coming to check out what was making the sound as he would be to the ruffians out there in the forest.

He had no choice.

Tyana's ears might hear him and the unicorn could lead Steigan to him. He had to take the chance.

Martias began softly, making slight sounds with his mouth. He paused, waiting between calls to listen. The forest remained quiet, except for a couple of birds which responded to him. They were no good.

He tried again, this time a little louder. Please, someone had to hear him. He'd even take a centaur. How much more humiliated could he possibly be? It no longer mattered who found him just as long as he didn't become a slave.

"Shh!" The sharp sound came from close by.

"Is someone there?" Martias called out.

"Shh! Shh!" Each shush came quicker and more agitated. "You must quiet all the noise. Be like me. Silent." After this, there came a low, cracking cackle.

"Can you help me?" Martias said, trying to keep his voice just barely above a whisper.

The branches started to shake nearby and Martias craned his neck to see if someone approached.

"Not a dominus, are you? Can't help you if you're a dominus."

"I'm not," Martias replied quickly.

"But you came from New Lilinar?"

"I did."

"Not a dominus?"

"No. I'm training to be a sapere?"

The man's dark eyes widened. "A centaur for a sapere?"

"Can you untie this rope?"

The man seemed to take forever walking around Martias and examining the situation. A wooden walking staff thumped against the ground in irregular beats. "Not sure I want to. Spent days leading them after you."

"You made those men follow us?"

The man smiled and licked his tongue against the back of his yellowing teeth. The deep brown of his tongue poked through the gapes were there were no teeth. "Kill a dominus. Always fun."

Fear settled into Martias' stomach. "Is my friend dead? Did they kill him? Is that why he isn't here now?"

The man dropped to his knees beside Martias and shoved a finger into the centaur's stomach. "Never be friends with a dominus. They will betray you every chance they get. Got it!"

Martias nodded. "Can we see about untying me now?"

The man squat on his feet. It didn't look too much different than his walking position except that he was closer to the ground now. He shuffled toward the tree to look at the ropes. "Expert knot. Those Plenelians sure do know how to tie them."

"You'll be able to undo it, right?"

"Possibly. Old hands don't work like they used to."

"I know you don't like domini very much, but if you just went to get my fr-- the dominus with me, he has a dagger that he can use--"

"No domini! I told you. Treacherous demons they. Don't trust!"

"Oh, no, I wouldn't dream of trusting a dominus, but this one has a sharp dagger."

"The better to stab you through the heart with."

Martias wanted to say that Steigan wouldn't do that, but

this man would never except the words as truth. Better to go along with the crazy man and hope that Steigan would return soon and chase him off. "The knots...can you untie them?"

The man reached out and tugged on the rope. "They are secure. Let those men come back for you."

"Why? Why would you do that? Why won't you let me go now?"

"Are you a sapere yet?"

"Yes. I've passed the initiation."

"What rank?"

"Fifth." Martias hated the desperation he heard in his own voice as he spoke the word.

"Fifth," the old man repeated as he placed a hand on Martias' shoulder. "Hold tight. The goddess you seek sleeps beneath the Temple. Let her guide you. She can help you with your magic."

"I don't understand."

The man leaned close now and spoke in Martias' ear. "They told me I didn't have magic either, but I did. I still do. Cazidor."

A flash blazed up around Martias and he shrieked as he felt a moment of heat against his chest and face. The man chuckled. The instant Martias felt the singed rope fall away from him, he shoved himself up and got to his feet, shaking dirt, leaves, and the odd sensations from him.

"Find your goddess there. She knows. She's trying to help your magic. Higher rank and you will find out." As the man spoke, he pushed himself up out of the seated position, but it happened with struggle as if he feared his bones might break in the process.

Martias grabbed the walking staff the man had been using and handed it back to him. "Who are you?"

"Don't recognize me?"

"Should I?"

"I suppose not. Long time since my portrait was painted. Hermiting in the sands, at least until I felt the flash of magic and knew it was time to start a war."

"You urged the Plenelians to attack New Lilinar?"

"I did no such thing."

"You just said you started the war."

"Shh! There you go being loud again. Shh!" The elder whacked Martias with the walking stick.

"Sorry. You are just making no sense."

"Sense is for idiots. Nothing is supposed to make sense. Greater mystery. Makes people have faith that way. You know that, training to be a sapere."

"You have magic? You can feel magic?"

The old man started chuckling between broken sentences. "Have magic? Wasn't supposed to. It was a mark... mark faded. Funny, huh? Can burn things now. Had I known... set him on fire."

"What are you going on about?"

"Not what... who. Yes, who. The saint. The Bloody Saint. Oh. Oh. He's got to be dead. No, he's dead. Can't possibly be alive. They said he'd come back for my sister. Not dead he won't. I'll burn him. Burn him!"

"Thank you for freeing me. I appreciate it." Martias took several slow steps backwards as he spoke hoping not to draw too much attention to himself.

The elder man hobbled after him with surprising swiftness. "Tell me... tell me, is the saint alive? Now that I'm out, can I get my revenge? Do you know if Saint Steigan still lives?"

Chills moved through Martias at hearing his friend's name. "No, I don't know if he's alive. I've never heard of him, so I suppose not."

"Warn the Temple. Magic. H-he could be back. Tell them

Holy Sapere Tanold sends the message. They will understand."

"I'll do that." Martias extricated himself from the hold the man took on him.

"We have allies. Come, come. I show you." The man started to hobble off, waving madly with the walking stick to urge Martias after him.

Martias followed, but he looked around hoping that Steigan was somewhere nearby and could get him away from this crazy man.

"I'm old, but this is older. Way older." Tanold lopped along faster as he approached the edge of a cave Martias could barely see the mouth of off through the trees. "Don't worry. He sleeps, like I did. Good sleep. Very pretty. You'll see."

Martias lingered at the edge of the cave, wondering how far inside this man would have to go to let Martias run away. If the lands were flat and his ankle not already injured, making a run for it would be easy. As it stood, even a hobbling old man could catch up to Martias easily.

"Come. It's safe." Tanold reached out of the shadows and grasped Martias' wrist. Though it shocked Martias, the feeble tug wasn't enough to drag him forward. Yet the soft sound of wind coming from inside was enough to tempt Martias into the venture of going to see what the old man wanted him to see.

Martias entered the cave. It didn't take long for his eyes to adjust to the dim light which radiated from the center of the room.

A huge beast of shimmering white glowed as it slept curled in a tight coil. Its long tail wrapped along the length of its body all the way up to its head.

"Our ally. He will help us to destroy Saint Steigan if he

comes for the goddess sleeping beneath the Temple. You will tell the other saperes?"

"I will." Martias moved around the creature whose head was larger than he stood tall.

"Swear!"

Martias jumped at the man's yell, half afraid he'd waked the beast. "I swear I will tell the saperes."

"No! Swear your loyalty to our sleeping friend."

"I swear to be loyal to him."

Tanold pointed a crooked finger toward the creature. "Nay, put your hands on him and swear!"

Martias put a hand on the sparkling hide of its shoulder. "I swear to be loyal to you." He hoped no one would ever hold him to that.

As he went to draw away, he felt a surge go through him and it stung his palm. He pulled his hand in quickly toward his body and held it.

"Centaur," the beast muttered in its sleep followed by a sound that could have been a chuckle.

"He likes you. Friend. He will make good ally. Tell saperes."

Martias wanted out, to get home. Yes, to the Temple. He might not be fully accepted there, but at least he knew he was safe.

Now that he'd seen this beast, was there anywhere that would be safe?

Martias moved toward the cave's mouth, longing for the forest beyond. Tanold followed as if ushering him out. Martias smelled the tang of ancient magic rising in the air.

Goddess, magic. Before, it had only been him. Now, Martias had discovered that others had it too.

He wanted out of the cave, wanted to feel the forest breeze against his face rather than his body responding to this magic.

"Wait!" The elder's eyes grew wide and he looked down at his feet. "Wait! No. I can't go back. Don't let it take me." Tanold dove for Martias, who evaded the grasp. His hooves kicked up some of the dark, earthy loam, sprinkling black dirt over the mossy undergrowth covering the cave floor.

The elderly man seemed to be shrinking as if pulled by something behind him and his legs were now made of smoke. He plunged his stick into the ground as if it were a stave which would keep him where he was, but his knobby fingers lost their grip on the branch. He made pitiful mewlings as he tried not to get dragged backwards. His eyes searched wildly for help as he clawed the air and tried to reach for Martias.

Martias shrank back, watching the man get helplessly pulled toward the ground. Only after Tanold had disappeared with a faint, sucking pop, did Martias move toward the spot where he saw a spout extended from beneath the moss and soft earth.

Martias reached for the abandoned walking stick and poked the shiny gold tube.

Nothing happened.

He knocked it again with the end of the stick, this time a little harder, and the loam rocked enough that Martias could see there was something buried there. He glanced around, wondering where Steigan had gotten to and wishing his friend would return. Now would be good.

But the cave and forest outside remained silent.

Martias used the stick to shake additional dirt free from the buried object, soon revealing a sort of teapot. It looked similar to the ones that Steigan's ma, Lucinia, owned except that this had an extensive curved spout and seemed to have been elongated. Martias hesitated to pick it up, but he used a ring toward the back to insert the stick and drag it out of the hole.

Settling his forelegs down on the ground, he bent over, nearly overextending himself, as he went to blow dust off. The odd, brown shape of his reflection moved over the shiny surface. He wasn't certain if he wanted to touch it anymore. What if he got pulled into it like Tanold had? How could a human, even as aged and shrunken as Tanold, fit inside such a tiny object?

Magic.

Another shiver went through Martias.

He couldn't let anyone find this object. The being inside the lamp had helped him, yes, but... magic was dangerous. He knew that firsthand.

Taking the stick, Martias dug out the hole where the lamp had been. Still not touching it with his hands and only using the stick to maneuver the teapot, Martias shoved it into the hole and began pushing the dirt over it. When he had a good layer, he pressed it down, flattening the land, pressing the plant's roots in solid, and making it look like nothing rested beneath.

Then he stood, stepped back a couple paces, and stared at the spot wondering if whatever existed with in the teapot could breathe buried as it was. Had he just killed whatever lay inside? Death might be welcomed rather than the further ravages of time on the mind and body of Tanold. There was a cycle to all things and that included life and death. If the being inside had lived beyond normal expectations, then death had a right to its due.

"Goddess," Martias said, beginning to whisper a prayer, but he didn't know if it was for himself or for Tanold. Both maybe.

There was also the glowing creature inside the cave. Martias wished he could forget about that too. But looking into the dark depths, he couldn't see any light emanating from within. Maybe the beast had been an illusion, something Tanold had wanted Martias to see in order to frighten him. He'd had enough fear for one day.

Rapidly, the thoughts of the Plenelians returning for him came, and Martias knew he had to leave. With luck, they would not accidentally stumble upon this area as they searched for the missing centaur. All Martias knew was that he now needed to get moving and the sooner he did the more time he'd have to cover his tracks.

With that, Martias left the gold teapot behind.

Martias took a careful spiral out from where he'd started until he found the signs he knew Steigan had left for him. Why had Steigan taken off? Had he heard the Plenelian men approach their camp and slipped off? But why was he leaving trail markings now? So many questions and Martias would only get answers when he caught up to Steigan. He added his own signals, a leaf bent in half, along the way in case Steigan was circling back. It made Martias keep a slight watch out to his left. He continued walking on throughout the day, making slow progress on his sore ankle.

"What were you thinking?" a familiar voice stated in a low, controlled boom a short distance away.

"I... I... I just..." came Steigan's broken voice.

"Quit stammering at me, boy. Don't you realize that you could be killed out here?"

The words seemed as if they could be concerned, but the tone behind them lacked true emotion. Martias knew in that moment that Steigan spoke to Dominus Greytas.

"Is Arlyn with you?" Steigan asked.

"No. Haven't seen him in nearly a month. We've started to wonder if he deserted."

"Arlyn wouldn't do that and you know it."

Martias saw them through the trees just in time for Greytas to give a sly smile to Steigan. "Wouldn't he?" Greytas asked with a taunt. "Got a little boy waiting back at home, or he should if you weren't standing here in front of me. Do you realize the danger you put us in too?"

"I'm sorry."

"We almost attacked you!" Greytas leaned forward to shout in Steigan's face. "We thought you were a Plenelian."

Greytas kept saying we as if there were multiple people there, but he could only see Greytas. If there were more, where were they? Martias moved to the side, trying carefully to see if there was anyone else hidden out in the trees, or maybe just beyond where Greytas and Steigan stood. He did see one other person, someone not unexpected, but just as unwelcomed as Greytas: Dominus Brynne. What a lovely day this was shaping up to be, Martias thought sarcastically.

"I'm sorry," Steigan repeated, though Martias was pretty certain that Greytas would never accept any apology.

"Blasted fool." Greytas pivoted and took a couple steps away from Steigan. "We can't leave you out here, but we can't take you back to camp either. What are we going to do with you?"

"I will head back to New Lilinar now. If Arlyn isn't with you, then I have no reason to be here."

Greytas leaned forward slightly as he yelled at Steigan. "You had no right to be here in the first place! Do you honestly believe I'm going to let you go traipsing out of here as if nothing happened?"

"No, sir, I don't suppose you will."

"At least you understand something," Greytas mocked with a wild flap of his arms as if he were giving up hope.

"I say if he wants to be here, we should let him pull his weight," Brynne offered. "We've got lots of supplies to carry."

Steigan remained defensive. "I will return to the Temple. Really! I just had a bad feeling about Arlyn and wanted to find out if he was all right. It's my only reason for being here." He sounded very much like the young boy he was.

Martias glanced around, wondering why Steigan was trying to leave the domini when they might very well be lying to him about Arlyn's whereabouts. If Steigan stayed with them, even temporarily, he'd find out more about Arlyn. But Steigan seemed only to want to get away.

Was he worried about having left Martias behind? So far, Martias realized that his name hadn't been mentioned. Maybe Steigan hadn't told the domini that Martias had actually been the one to lead them out here.

But there seemed to be even more than that.

Steigan's hands were tight at his sides as if he put all his energy into his clenched fists to keep from moving about impatiently. What else was going on?

Then Martias realized Tyana wasn't there. Steigan had left the unicorn behind. The Plenelians could have her too.

Martias backed away as quietly as he could from his spot among the dense branches. Steigan would figure this situation out on his own. But Tyana, she could be in real danger. For Steigan's sake, Martias would go and find her.

After he'd made it far enough away that he felt he could begin to hurry without being heard, Martias turned and rushed deeper into the forest. When he stopped, he listened and looked for signs that someone or something had been through here.

It didn't take him long before he found his own broken leaves from his trail. Shortly, he found Steigan's markers. If he traced them back, he was bound to find the unicorn. Unless it wasn't until Steigan had discovered Greytas and Brynne that he had released Tyana and tried to hide her away.

Martias looked back over his shoulder, second-guessing his direction. Which way should he go?

Why had Steigan left camp to begin with? If only Martias knew the answer to that question, he might be able to figure out where he needed to go now. Would Steigan have taken Tyana with him, or left her behind?

Steigan had left Martias behind.

Yes, Steigan would have left Tyana too, wanting to be able to sneak up on whatever he'd heard that had spurred him to leave camp. Chances were good that Steigan hadn't felt like they were in danger, or he would have woken Martias. Unless the people were so close that Steigan feared any sound being heard.

He didn't have time to stand here and try to figure this out with logic. He had to make a choice. Steigan had left camp. That was a simple fact. Would he have taken Tyana or not? A simple enough question, but with too many complex variables that Martias couldn't even begin to guess at.

He just had to make a choice.

Steigan had left a trail.

He had meant for Martias to catch up.

Tyana wouldn't understand how to track. She was young too, nearly helpless and weak. Steigan would leave her behind.

But that didn't mean she hadn't followed him.

That thought pushed Martias to take the trail away from camp. Tyana had followed. She wouldn't understand that she was to stay behind for Martias to keep safe. She would want to remain with Steigan. He had to have known this. Which meant he'd take the unicorn with him in order to keep her from getting lost. But somewhere along the way, Steigan had hidden her.

Martias began to look for signs he hoped Steigan had left for him to find Tyana. Maybe Steigan had even left his own breadcrumb trail, knowing he might need to find his way back.

Martias rushed along. "Where did he leave you?" He glanced side to side, trying to scope out all the underbrush where a young unicorn could have been hidden. "Why did he leave you?"

The thought seemed to make Martias overtly aware that something had scared Steigan. If it had just been the Plenelians, Steigan would have stayed with her. These were his own people Steigan was hiding the unicorn from.

Or was there more?

What else could have...

Martias stopped, but his heart continued to thunder in his chest so hard that he could feel it in his neck and ears.

Steigan had been following the unicorn. Tyana had left the camp first, not Steigan. She had led him away from the danger of the Plenelians' approach.

"And she left me," Martias added, trying not to feel bitterness, but it wasn't working.

He hated this, not knowing and merely having to surmise what had happened. He wanted facts. Yet as he cast his gaze around once more to still find no signs of anyone having come through here, he couldn't discard the feelings of having been abandoned. It made Martias want to head down the mountain now and leave Steigan behind to his fate with the others.

But it wasn't Steigan's fault that Martias had once again been left behind. No, that chain had started with the centaurs leaving him at the Temple.

Martias kicked at a stone on the ground, sending it skittering down the mountainside. This whole trip had done nothing but remind him about how his centaur family had deserted him.

He rubbed his hand, realizing as he did so that he felt the remnants of his dying brother holding onto him and begging him not to leave. No one wanted to be lonely.

He now felt homesick. Not for his centaur tribe, but for the Temple at New Lilinar. Life wasn't perfect there. Okay, he down right hated it. He felt different, out of place, mocked, yet he also knew perfect calm and silence there. The saperes had such a stillness to their lives. Repetitious, yes, but still nevertheless. They brought that feeling to hurting people when a loved one died. While they often shared in life's celebrations, they also remained there for the people that got left behind. No one ever had to feel abandoned.

He would think no more of the banishment from his centaur tribe or of the magic that had caused it. He'd leave that curse in the past. From now on, he'd reach to be a better person and make himself into what he wanted to be.

Martias felt a sensation growing in his chest. This had been such a strange trip. Yet at this moment he knew he would go back to New Lilinar and make sure no one would ever feel alone again. That was his mission.

It started with not leaving Steigan. He'd lead his friend out of here.

Tyana stepped from behind some bushes and looked up at him with her wide, dark eyes.

"You know my decision, don't you?" he asked.

She merely blinked.

"Is Arlyn alive?" Martias asked. "Are you here to make sure that Steigan is not alone?" He realized after he asked the question that there was no way the unicorn could understand him, if she knew if Arlyn was alive or not, or that he and Steigan had been friends for so long that neither one of them would ever be abandoned. "Are you alone?"

She blinked again.

"Not anymore. Come on. I have one more thing to do."

Martias hurried through the forest, following his trail back to the cave. He turned frequently along the way to make sure that the unicorn followed him. After digging up the strange looking teapot and brushing off the dust, he stuck it in his pack. No one should ever be alone, not even the crazy man stuck in the lamp who claimed that he'd once been a Holy Sapere. He should be at the Temple. Martias would return him home.

He noticed the unicorn watching him. "You won't tell Steigan about this, right? This will be our little secret?"

The unicorn nickered and gave a tilt of her head. Martias took that as an agreement.

"Let's go get Steigan and go home."

Three cycles later, Martias stood near the stables with the gamekeeper as they watched Steigan taking his first ride on Tyana. The unicorn's hooves clattered as she galloped across the bridge to the Temple.

"Still don't know how he does it," Kadlyn said, shaking his head. He leaned with his back against the fence. "Every day, Steigan just comes to stand by the edge of the stables and she saunters out of the forest as if she's been waiting all night for him."

"She's smart," Martias responded.

"I'm also amazed that he had the patience to wait to ride her. Seems that unicorns grow just a touch faster than horses, but he wanted to wait just to make sure."

Martias smiled with a little snicker. "I think keeping Steigan from gaining his title an extra year probably had something to do with his patience."

"I hear you'll be elevating within the season, Sapere Martias. Moving to the third rank. Getting close to the top. You think you'll reach for the brass ring when you get there?"

Grinning, Martias swept back his long wavy brown hair with his fingers and kept his hand on his head for just a moment longer. "What? Me becoming the Holy Sapere? I don't think they want a centaur in that position."

"Hey, you never know what the Goddess intends for us."

Steigan bolted with Tyana back across the bridge from the Temple, sparing them a brief wave as unicorn and rider bound down the road to head deeper into New Lilinar.

"My friend is the one bound for greatness," Martias said, bending forward. He placed his chin down on his arms folded over the top board of the wooden fence. "I'm just a sapere, looking to be as helpful to the Goddess' people as I can be."

Steigan now had Tyana racing back down along the road, this time toward the houses on the north end, those closest to the old ruins of Lilinar.

In his wake, several children came running up to Martias and the gamekeeper. "Sapere Martias," one of the boys shouted, "will you come help us?"

Martias pushed back from the fence. "What do you need?"

"Shalen wants a story, but we all have to finish our letters and our numbers first. You're the only one who can help us with our homework and then tell us a good enough story that Shalen will be quiet."

"Yeah," piped up one of the other boys. "The other saperes only tell us boring stories. You have good ones!"

"All right. Where did you leave your books? Hopefully not by the shoreline again." Martias wasn't really paying attention as they answered. A couple of the kids ran off in search of their books. Martias turned to Kadlyn. "Will you tell Dominus Steigan where I went off to? He might need to come rescue me from this horde."

"Will do, Sapere Martias. Have fun."

As Martias started to walk off with the remaining children all dancing excitedly around him, the gamekeeper called to him once more. "Oh, and Martias? Dominus Steigan might be bound for greatness, but you are the rare individual walking a unique path. Many would have been bound by the judgments of others, but you open yourself to compassion. That makes you exceptional."

An exception to the centaurs. Martias smiled. One of the boys reached out and grabbed onto Martias' wrist, urging him along faster. "Thank you," Martias called back to the gamekeeper. Then he was off to help the children.

※

Join the Quest for the Three Books now.

The courage to become legendary:

Discover the magic in the epic fantasy adventure of Sacred Knight

When helping a princess to find three lost books, he never expected to make such enemies.

The Missing Thread (Book 5) coming soon!

About the Author

Dawn Blair grew up on a ranch in a rural Nevada town. The old buildings provided inspiration for her imagination as she thrived on stories of unicorns, princesses, heroic knights, and hidden doors to other dimensions.

For as long as she can remember, Dawn has had a passion for storytelling. Though she started out writing, her creative life expanded into painting and illustration.

She loves creating worlds and spinning tales for people to enjoy. The best ones are the stories that surprise her as she's writing. She loves her characters doing the unexpected. She'll gladly tell you that the most exciting part about being a writer is being the first one on the journey.

Thank you for taking the time to join her on these adventures.

Find more about Dawn and her work at:
www.dawnblair.com

facebook.com/dawnblairbooks
twitter.com/dawnblair
instagram.com/dawn.blair

Made in the USA
Columbia, SC
16 March 2021